Table of Contents

Many Colors

Tim is at the market.

Healthy Living

Vegetables

by Vanessa Black

Bullfrog Books

Ideas for Parents and Teachers

Bullfrog Books let children practice reading informational text at the earliest reading levels. Repetition, familiar words, and photo labels support early readers.

Before Reading

- Discuss the cover photo. What does it tell them?
- Look at the picture glossary together. Read and discuss the words.

Read the Book

- "Walk" through the book and look at the photos. Let the child ask questions. Point out the photo labels.
- Read the book to the child, or have him or her read independently.

After Reading

- Prompt the child to think more. Ask: How many servings of vegetables do you think you eat a day? What is your favorite vegetable?

Bullfrog Books are published by Jump!
5357 Penn Avenue South
Minneapolis, MN 55419
www.jumplibrary.com

Library of Congress Cataloging-in-Publication Data

Names: Black, Vanessa, author.
Title: Vegetables / by Vanessa Black.
Description: Minneapolis, MN: Jump!, Inc. [2017]
Series: Healthy living
"Bullfrog Books are published by Jump!."
Audience: Ages 5–8. | Audience: K to grade 3.
Includes bibliographical references and index.
Identifiers: LCCN 2016029312 (print)
LCCN 2016031889 (ebook)
ISBN 9781620315484 (hardcover: alk. paper)
ISBN 9781620315828 (pbk.)
ISBN 9781624964961 (ebook)
Subjects: LCSH: Vegetables in human nutrition —Juvenile literature.
Vegetables—Juvenile literature.
Classification: LCC QP144.V44 B53 2017 (print)
LCC QP144.V44 (ebook) | DDC 613.2—dc23
LC record available at https://lccn.loc.gov/2016029312

Editor: Jenny Fretland VanVoorst
Book Designer: Molly Ballanger
Photo Researcher: Molly Ballanger

Photo Credits: All photos by Shutterstock except: age fotostock, 16–17, 23tl; iStock, 10–11; Niloo/Shutterstock.com, 23bl; Thinkstock, 8, 20–21.

Printed in the United States of America at Corporate Graphics in North Mankato, Minnesota.

Wow!

Look at all the vegetables.

Look at all the colors.

Red. Green. White.
Purple. Orange.

Eat them all.

Look! Kira has carrots.

They have vitamin A.
It is good for your eyes.

spinach

Rima has spinach.

It has iron.

It is good for the blood.

Zoe has broccoli.

It has vitamin C.

It is good
for the skin.

sweet
potato

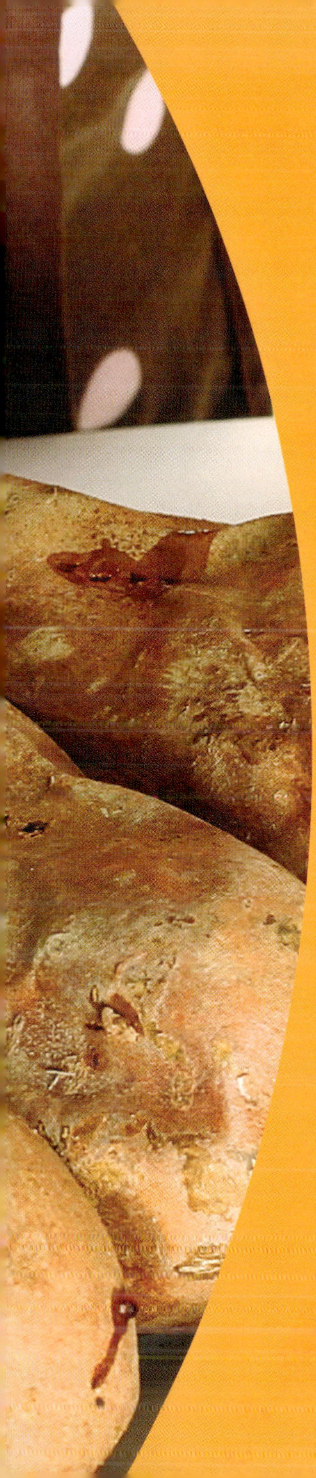

Pia has sweet potatoes.
They have vitamin D.
It is good for your bones.

chard

Look! Ava has chard.

It has vitamin K.

It is good for your heart.

Mo makes a salad.

She cuts.

She chops.

Yum!

Veggies are good!

Your Daily Vegetables

You need at least three servings of vegetables a day.

carrots
A sweet, crunchy root vegetable with orange skin.

cauliflower
A garden plant grown for its compact, edible head of white, undeveloped flowers.

green onions
The small, white bulbs of green onions have a milder flavor than that of other onions.

Brussels sprouts
The small, compact bud of a variety of cabbage.

Picture Glossary

chard
A leafy green vegetable with colorful stems.

salad
A mix of vegetables usually eaten cold.

iron
A metal your body needs to stay healthy.

sweet potato
The sweet, starchy root of a flowering vine.

market
A place to buy food.

vitamin
Something in food that people need to stay healthy.

Index

To Learn More

Learning more is as easy as 1, 2, 3.

1) Go to www.factsurfer.com
2) Enter "vegetables" into the search box.
3) Click the "Surf" button to see a list of websites.

With factsurfer.com, finding more information is just a click away.